Contents

Warrior Kings ... 4

Long Live the King! ... 6

Coronation! ... 8

Royal Rights (and Wrongs) ... 10

A Modern Monarch ... 12

Parades and Pageantry ... 14

Palaces Galore ... 16

Buckingham Palace ... 18

The Royal Court ... 20

A Knight's Tale ... 21

Royal Patrons ... 22

Royal Trades ... 24

Family of Nations ... 26

A Working Queen ... 28

Around Royal London ... 30

Index and Quiz Answers ... 32

Warrior Kings

Hundreds of years ago, Britain didn't have just one king — it had lots! Celtic kings and princes ruled Scotland, Ireland and Wales, and everything else was divided up between tribes of Anglo-Saxons.

Each tribe had its own king. Sometimes one king became more powerful than the others, and for a while he would be an overlord or chief king.

Then, in the early 800s, bands of Danish Vikings from northern Europe began attacking Britain.

One day, King Canute was walking on the bank of the River Thames at Westminster and got his feet wet. His servants said that he was such a great king he could order the tide to turn back. To show them how foolish they were Canute did so. Of course, the Thames went on rising until the king was soaked to his knees.

Divide and rule

In 878, the Saxon King of Wessex, Alfred the Great, won a great battle against the Danes and forced them to agree to peace. Much of Britain was divided into Danish land (the Danelaw) and Anglo-Saxon land (England).

Gradually Danes and Saxons learned to live together, and in 924 Athelstan (Alfred's grandson) became king of both Saxon and Danish lands — the first 'King of England'. But England wasn't peaceful for long. After about 60 years, the Viking raids began again — and only ended in 1016, when the Danish king, Canute, became King of England.

A Rich Prize

Because it is on the River Thames, London became a wealthy trading port in Saxon times. But the river brought the Vikings too, who wanted London's wealth for themselves and were always looting and burning the town.

By the 850s, London had been raided so many times it was virtually abandoned.

In 880, King Alfred of Wessex rebuilt London and made it strong again. But it wasn't until Canute became king that London was finally safe from Viking raids.

ABOUT 700 BC CELTIC TRIBES ARRIVE IN BRITAIN FROM EUROPE

FROM AD 400s ANGLO-SAXON TRIBES INVADE AND SETTLE IN BRITAIN

871–899 ALFRED THE GREAT IS KING OF WESSEX

Royal London

FROM ALFRED THE GREAT TO ELIZABETH II

by Jacqui Bailey

A & C BLACK • LONDON

The London String of Pearls Golden Jubilee Festival

Many of the buildings in this book are part of the 'String of Pearls'. This is a collection of important buildings (some famous and some you may never have heard of) that are threaded together by the River Thames, like pearls on a string.

Over the centuries these buildings have played a key part in our history and many continue to do so today. They all have connections with Royalty, and to celebrate the Queen's Golden Jubilee in 2002 they are throwing open their doors and putting on hundreds of special tours, displays, concerts and other events for you to explore.

If you would like a full programme of the Festival events in 2002, send a cheque for £2 (payable to String of Pearls) together with your name and address to: London String of Pearls, P.O. Box 967, Aylesford, Kent ME20 7UP.

With thanks to the Museum of London for their help in preparing this book.

First published in 2002 by A & C Black Publishers Limited,
37 Soho Square, London W1D 3QZ
www.acblack.com
in association with The London String of Pearls

ISBN 0-7136-6261-1

Printed in Hong Kong
by Wing King Tong Limited

Created for A & C Black Limited by
two's COMPANY
Designed by Matthew Lilly
Illustrations by Tony Kenyon/B L Kearley;
Matthew Lilly; Ian Thompson; Peter Visscher
Cover illustrations by Clive Goodyear/
Pennant Illustration Agency (figures);
Matthew Lilly (spots); Peter Visscher (scenes)

The Publishers would also like to thank the following for permission to use their photographs and paintings:
Barnard & Westwood Ltd (p24l); Camera Press (p13); Collections/Brian Shuel (p24); Collections/Yuri Lewinski (p22t); Commonwealth Institute (p27b); Coram Foundation, Foundling Museum, London, UK/Bridgeman Art Library (p25); Guildhall Art Gallery, Corporation of London, UK/Bridgeman Art Library (p14r); London Aerial Photo Library (pp18-19); London String of Pearls Golden Jubilee Festival (pp1, 15b, 16l, 17t, 17r, 21b); Press Association News Photographic Library (pp 6, 9, 12, 14l, 15t, 16r, 17l, 18t, 20, 21t, 22b, 23b, 27t, 28-29); The Royal Collection © HM Queen Elizabeth II (pp8, 23t).

Rulers of England

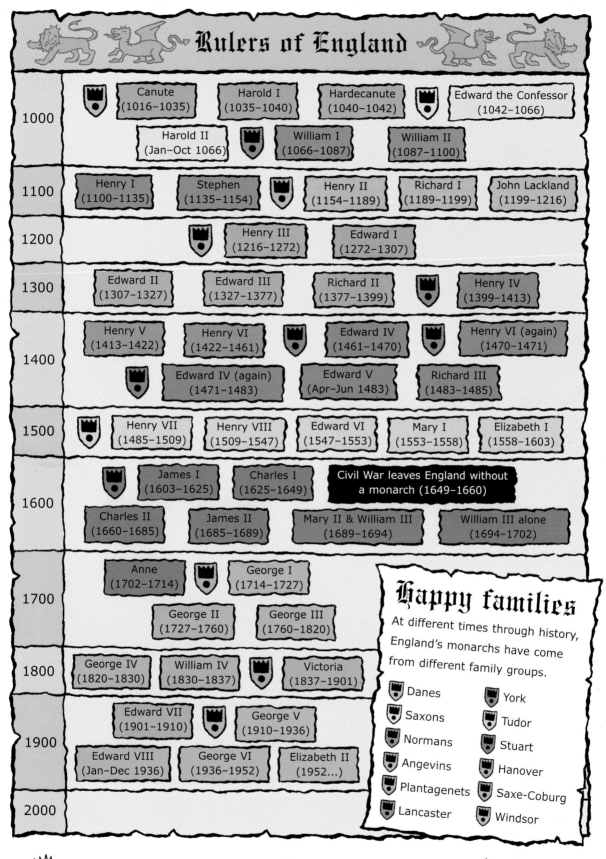

| 1000 | Canute (1016–1035) | Harold I (1035–1040) | Hardecanute (1040–1042) | Edward the Confessor (1042–1066) |

Harold II (Jan–Oct 1066) · William I (1066–1087) · William II (1087–1100)

| 1100 | Henry I (1100–1135) | Stephen (1135–1154) | Henry II (1154–1189) | Richard I (1189–1199) | John Lackland (1199–1216) |

| 1200 | Henry III (1216–1272) | Edward I (1272–1307) |

| 1300 | Edward II (1307–1327) | Edward III (1327–1377) | Richard II (1377–1399) | Henry IV (1399–1413) |

| 1400 | Henry V (1413–1422) | Henry VI (1422–1461) | Edward IV (1461–1470) | Henry VI (again) (1470–1471) |

Edward IV (again) (1471–1483) · Edward V (Apr–Jun 1483) · Richard III (1483–1485)

| 1500 | Henry VII (1485–1509) | Henry VIII (1509–1547) | Edward VI (1547–1553) | Mary I (1553–1558) | Elizabeth I (1558–1603) |

| 1600 | James I (1603–1625) | Charles I (1625–1649) | **Civil War leaves England without a monarch (1649–1660)** |

Charles II (1660–1685) · James II (1685–1689) · Mary II & William III (1689–1694) · William III alone (1694–1702)

| 1700 | Anne (1702–1714) | George I (1714–1727) |

George II (1727–1760) · George III (1760–1820)

| 1800 | George IV (1820–1830) | William IV (1830–1837) | Victoria (1837–1901) |

| 1900 | Edward VII (1901–1910) | George V (1910–1936) |

Edward VIII (Jan–Dec 1936) · George VI (1936–1952) · Elizabeth II (1952...)

| 2000 | |

Happy families

At different times through history, England's monarchs have come from different family groups.

- Danes
- Saxons
- Normans
- Angevins
- Plantagenets
- Lancaster
- York
- Tudor
- Stuart
- Hanover
- Saxe-Coburg
- Windsor

899–1016 ALFRED'S DESCENDENTS MORE OR LESS RULE ENGLAND

1016–1035 CANUTE IS KING OF ALL ENGLAND

1035–1040 HAROLD I, CANUTE'S ILLEGITIMATE SON, IS KING

Long Live the King!

William the Conqueror died from a battle wound in France in 1087. The story goes that the instant he was dead his servants stripped his body and left him. Eventually his rotting corpse was found, but when it was squashed into a too-small tomb it exploded and sent everyone running.

Today, when a king or queen dies the crown usually passes to the eldest son, or if there are no sons it goes to the eldest daughter. But in the Middle Ages, if a king had no sons then other powerful nobles might claim the throne.

A royal battle

In 1066, the lack of a son led to the Battle of Hastings. King Edward (the Confessor) had no children and when he died his throne was claimed by two lords — the Saxon earl, Harold Godwinson, and William, Duke of Normandy in France.

Edward's council of nobles chose Harold to be king, but William decided to fight for the throne. William's Norman soldiers defeated Harold's Saxons, and William 'the Conqueror' became King of England.

The Tower of London

William built lots of castles around England and filled them with soldiers to stop the Saxons rebelling. The traders of London were both rich and argumentative, so he built three castle towers in London to make sure they stayed loyal to him.

THE TOWER OF LONDON is the only one still standing. Later kings added more bits to it and it has been used as a fortress, a prison, a treasury, and even a royal zoo! All sorts of wild animals, from leopards to polar bears, were kept there. Today, the only wild animals that live in the Tower are the ravens. Legend has it that if the ravens ever leave, the Tower will collapse and so will the monarchy.

1040–1042
HARDECANUTE,
CANUTE'S
LEGITIMATE
SON, IS KING

1042–1066
EDWARD (THE
CONFESSOR)
IS ON THE
THRONE

JAN–OCT 1066
HAROLD II IS
THE LAST
SAXON KING

Grabbing a throne

William wasn't the only king to take the throne by force. A king could lose his throne if he was weak or ruled badly.

Richard III, for example, grabbed the throne in 1483 after imprisoning his young nephew, Edward V. But he didn't keep it for long.

Not everyone was happy with his rule, and in 1485 Henry Tudor, the Earl of Richmond, defeated Richard III in battle and became Henry VII, the first of a line of Tudor rulers.

Richard III was chopped to pieces by Henry's knights at the Battle of Bosworth Field. He was the last English king to be killed on a battlefield.

Queens for kings

Women were thought to be too weak to rule on their own. When Matilda, the only child of Henry I, claimed the throne in 1135 the nobles chose her cousin Stephen instead.

The first woman to rule England in her own right was Mary I, in 1553. She was the eldest daughter of Henry VIII and when Henry's son died at the age of 16, Mary was chosen to be Queen.

Mary I had no children, and when she died the throne also went to a woman — her half-sister Elizabeth I.

In Search of a Son

Beheaded: Anne Boleyn. One child: Elizabeth I

Died: Jane Seymour. One child: Edward VI

Divorced: Anne of Cleeves. No children

Beheaded: Catherine Howard. No children

Divorced: Catherine of Aragon. One child: Mary I

Henry VIII was so desperate for a son that when his first wife had only one daughter he divorced her and married again. His second wife also had a daughter and she was executed. His third wife had a son, but she died two weeks later. Henry married three more times but had no more children. Of all his wives, he loved Jane Seymour the best and when he died her bones were placed alongside his.

Survived: Catherine Parr. Outlived Henry VIII

Coronation!

In 1066, Harold II and William the Conqueror were both crowned at **WESTMINSTER ABBEY** in London. They were the first Kings of England to be crowned there and every English monarch has been crowned there since. (Except for Edward V and Edward VIII, who didn't stay on the throne long enough to be crowned anywhere at all!)

St Edward's Crown has been used for every coronation since it was made in 1660. It is believed to contain gold melted down from Edward the Confessor's crown.

A Saintly Abbey

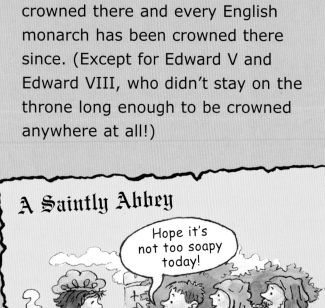

Hope it's not too soapy today!

WESTMINSTER ABBEY was built by Edward the Confessor, who died and was buried there in 1066. Edward was so religious people believed he could heal them, so his servants saved his bathwater and gave it to sick people to drink or to put in their eyes if they were blind.

After his death a number of miracles are said to have happened. In 1161 he was made a saint and a huge shrine was put in the abbey to contain his body. Today, Edward's shrine is the only one in the country that still holds the remains of its saint.

An ancient ceremony

A new king or queen begins to rule as soon as their succession to the throne has been announced. But the coronation — when the crown is placed on the monarch's head — may not happen until months later.

At the coronation ceremony the monarch swears an oath to rule according to the law, to give justice with mercy, and to uphold the Church. Then he or she sits on the Coronation Chair and is anointed with oils, and given a cloak of gold cloth to wear.

1100-1135 HENRY I IS ON THE THRONE

1135-1154 STEPHEN IS ON THE THRONE

1154-1189 HENRY II IS ON THE THRONE

Queen Elizabeth II was crowned at Westminster Abbey on 2 June, 1953, sixteen months after her accession to the throne on 6 February 1952. It was the first coronation ever to be shown on television.

Crowning glory

Next, the king or queen is given the objects that symbolise a monarch's power: a ring, a golden globe called the orb, two golden rods called sceptres — one of which holds the largest cut diamond in the world — and finally St Edward's Crown. All these precious objects are part of the collection known as the Crown Jewels and are kept in the Tower of London.

The first set of Crown Jewels belonged to Edward the Confessor. But they've changed a lot since then. King John is said to have dropped his in some quicksand in 1216. And Edward III pawned his for money to pay his soldiers.

An Uncrowned King

Boys? What boys?

In 1483, 13-year-old Edward V was king for just 11 weeks. Then his guardian and uncle, Richard III, locked him up in the Tower of London and took his place on the throne.

Later, the unfortunate Edward and his younger brother mysteriously disappeared. Rumour has it they were murdered and buried in the Tower.

1172 HENRY II BECOMES OVERLORD OF IRELAND

1189–1199 RICHARD I (THE LIONHEART) IS ON THE THRONE

Royal Rights (and Wrongs)

At first, King John refused to agree to *Magna Carta*. Then his nobles raised an army against him and he gave in. The Charter was finally approved on 15 June 1215 at Runnymede — a meadow beside the River Thames near Windsor Castle. More changes were added later and a copy of the final version of 1225 is kept at the PUBLIC RECORD OFFICE at Kew in London.

Long ago, monarchs had more power than they do today. They had a council of advisers to help them, but it was they who decided how the country was run and what laws were made. Most monarchs ruled reasonably fairly — until King John came to the throne in 1199. John lost wars abroad, argued with the Pope (the head of the Church in Rome) and demanded more taxes (money) from his nobles.

A great charter

The nobles and the church leaders became very angry and they drew up a list of the rights they wanted the king to give them. The list was called the *Magna Carta* (or Great Charter). Among other things, it said that the king must discuss all important decisions with his nobles, and they had the right to form a council to make sure that he kept his promises. When John agreed to the Charter it became law, and for the first time in history the king's power was limited by law.

What does he mean, "No"?

A Right Royal Quarrel

King John wasn't the only king to argue with the Pope. Henry VIII was a very religious man, but when the Pope refused to let him divorce his first wife in 1527, Henry was outraged.

In 1533, Henry declared that the English Church would no longer follow the leadership of the Pope in Rome. A year later a law was passed that made Henry VIII the 'Supreme Head of the Church of England'.

Today, the Queen is still the Head of the Church of England, although its spiritual leader is the Archbishop of Canterbury.

1199–1216
JOHN
(LACKLAND)
IS ON THE
THRONE

1215
KING JOHN
APPROVES
MAGNA CARTA

1216–1272
HENRY III
IS ON THE
THRONE

Death of a King

Charles I is the only English king ever to be executed. Charles fought against Parliament's army for seven years, but on 20 January 1649 he was put on trial at Westminster Palace for 'treason to his people'. Charles refused to defend himself and said that the trial was not legal. Many members of Parliament agreed with him, but the army insisted that the trial take place and Charles was found guilty.

It was a cold day on 30 January, and Charles asked for an extra shirt to wear in case the crowds thought he was shivering with fear. At 1pm he walked out of a window of the **BANQUETING HOUSE** at Whitehall Palace and onto a scaffold where he was executed.

GUESS WHAT? Who was the last king to lead troops into battle? a) Charles I b) George II c) George VI

Power to the Parliament

Magna Carta was the first of many steps that gradually lessened the monarch's power.

By the 1600s, the king's council had become known as 'Parliament' and it had grown to include wealthy merchants. They all wanted a say in how the country was run and particularly how the taxes were spent.

Kings and Queens often argued with their Parliaments over money, but the situation finally came to a head with Charles I.

Magna Carta wasn't signed by King John as he couldn't read or write. Instead he stamped it with his royal seal.

Civil war

In 1642, a civil war broke out between the King's supporters (the Cavaliers) and Parliament's (the Roundheads). Led by Oliver Cromwell, Parliament's army won and the monarchy was abolished. Now Parliament was ruled by Cromwell.

Cromwell's England was a gloomy place and after his death in 1658, Charles' son was invited back from France. In 1660 Charles II was crowned. The monarchy was restored, but its role had changed forever.

1272–1307
EDWARD I
(LONGSHANKS)
IS ON THE
THRONE

1282
EDWARD I IS FIRST
ENGLISH KING TO
TAKE CONTROL
OF WALES

A Modern Monarch

The Queen still has the right to reject laws made by Parliament, although no ruler has done so since the early 1700s.

NEW
It will be annou...
in Parliament that...
will come into for...
in the coming futu...
very much of cours...
majesty the Queen...
whole-heartedly. U...
time the new law will come...
into force and everyone will...
have to obey and conform to...
the new rule. That is of course...
that her majesty approves.
Signed

Today, Queen Elizabeth II is known as a 'constitutional monarch'. This means that although she is officially the head of the state, the country is actually run by the government, led by the Prime Minister.

The government is formed by the political group or 'party' that has the most members in the House of Commons. This is the part of Parliament whose members are chosen by public vote in a General Election. General Elections are held at least every five years.

Meeting royal approval

Although the monarch's power is limited, the Queen still has an important part to play. Different governments come and go, but the monarch remains the nation's representative.

A Royal Meeting Place

In William the Conqueror's time, the king's council would meet wherever the king was staying. Sometimes this was at Westminster.

Gradually the council or 'Parliament' grew too big to move around. In the 1300s, it split into two 'houses' — nobles and churchmen formed the 'House of Lords' and wealthy merchants formed the 'House of Commons'. When the king went on his travels, Parliament stayed at Westminster.

Westminster became the administrative centre of the kingdom, and in 1512 Henry VIII moved out of the Palace of Westminster and gave it to Parliament. Today, the palace is better known as the **HOUSES OF PARLIAMENT**, yet it is still officially a royal palace.

1307–1327
EDWARD II
IS KING UNTIL
HE IS KILLED
IN 1327

1327–1377
EDWARD III
IS ON THE
THRONE

1377–1399
RICHARD II
IS KING UNTIL
HE IS DEPOSED
IN 1399

The State Opening of Parliament

The State Opening of Parliament is the ceremony that officially marks the start of a new Parliamentary year. State Openings usually take place in November, or soon after a General Election. On the day of the Opening, the Queen travels to the Houses of Parliament in the State Coach and sits on the throne in the House of Lords. An official known as Black Rod then knocks on the door of the House of Commons to summon its members to the House of Lords. No king or queen has entered the House of Commons since 1642, when Charles I stormed in with his soldiers and tried to arrest five Members of Parliament who were there.

The Queen has both the right and the duty to offer advice to the government. She has to approve all new laws that Parliament wishes to make, and meets regularly with the Prime Minister to discuss the government's plans. She also carries out similar tasks for the Scottish Parliament and the Welsh and Northern Irish Assemblies.

At the start of every working day the Mace is carried into the chamber of the House of Commons. Without it, the House cannot officially begin to meet. Long ago, a mace was a weapon used to protect the monarch. Today it is a symbol of the power the monarch has given to the House of Commons.

1399–1413
HENRY IV (OF BOLINGBROKE) IS ON THE THRONE

1413–1422
HENRY V IS ON THE THRONE

1422–1461
HENRY VI IS KING UNTIL HE IS DEPOSED IN 1461

Parades and Pageantry

Royal rulers have long known that one of the best ways to please their subjects is to put on a good display of royal splendour.

Early kings moved around the country a lot with their households, their finery and their furniture, in a showy parade known as the Royal Progress.

By the 1300s, though, the Crown Jewels and the Royal Treasury were both stored at Westminster Palace and most of the day-to-day business of running the country took place there. So although the royal household still moved around quite a lot, London became the setting for all of the really major royal events.

One king who was always on the move was Henry VIII. He owned about 60 grand houses around the country and he liked to visit them all.

City celebrations

Today, royal births, weddings and many other special events still take place in London, although celebrations often happen in other parts of the country at the same time.

The Queen's Diamond Jubilee, 1897 by Andrew Carrick Gow (1848-1920)
Guildhall Art Gallery, Corporation of London, UK/Bridgeman Art Library

Left: 'Beefeaters', or Yeomen Warders, have guarded the Tower of London since the time of Henry VIII.

Above: Queen Victoria arrives at St Paul's Cathedral for a thanksgiving service during her Diamond Jubilee in 1897. The Jubilee marked 60 years of her reign and was celebrated in countries all over the world.

1461-1470
EDWARD IV
(EARL OF MARCH)
TAKES THE
THRONE

1470-1471
HENRY VI TAKES
IT BACK, IS
DEPOSED AGAIN
AND KILLED

1471-1483
EDWARD IV ON
THE THRONE
AGAIN

The Nation's Church

ST PAUL'S CATHEDRAL is in the heart of London. The first St Paul's was built in about AD 604, but it was rebuilt many times and the magnificent cathedral you can see today was finished in 1710.

St Paul's is called 'the nation's parish church', because it is where 'the great and the good' of England come to celebrate their marriages, bury their dead, and give thanks for the ending of wars.

Perhaps the most popular royal event to take place there in recent times was the marriage of Prince Charles to Lady Diana Spencer in 1981. The ceremony was shown on television and was watched by 750 million people all over the world.

Birthday colours

A royal event that takes place every year is the Trooping of the Colour on **HORSE GUARDS** Parade in **WHITEHALL**. This is when soldiers of the Foot Guards and the Household Cavalry parade ('troop') their regimental flags ('colours') in front of the Royal family and members of the public.

Originally the purpose of the parade was to make sure the troops recognised their own flags in battle. But since 1748, it has also marked the monarch's 'official' birthday. Monarchs have two birthdays — their real one and one which is publicly celebrated in the summer.

Queen Elizabeth II was born on 21 April but her official birthday is celebrated by the Trooping of the Colour in June.

Will you marry me?

According to royal rules, no man is allowed to ask a queen for her hand in marriage — she has to ask him. Queen Victoria was just a shy girl of 20 when she popped the question to Prince Albert.

JUNE 1483
EDWARD V IS
DEPOSED AFTER
ONLY 11 WEEKS
AS KING

1483–1485
RICHARD III
IS ON THE
THRONE

Palaces Galore

Kings and queens didn't only move around the country, they also liked to move around London. Because of this, London is littered with royal palaces.

Some palaces are more important than others, though. Kings or queens may stay in different palaces at different times of the year, but they usually spend most of their time in one particular palace and this is known as the 'official royal residence'. As well as being the monarch's home, the official residence is where most of the important royal ceremonies are held.

Edward the Confessor made the Palace of Westminster the first official London residence, but five hundred years later things changed...

Henry VIII turned Hampton Court into one of the most modern palaces in England.

It had tennis courts, bowling alleys, vast kitchens — and a multiple garderobe, or lavatory, called the 'Great House of Easement' which could seat 28 people at the same time.

WHITEHALL PALACE In 1529, Henry VIII got fed up with Westminster Palace and built himself a vast pile called Whitehall Palace. It covered 23 acres and it was the official residence until it burned down in 1698 (the road called Whitehall today was once the palace courtyard).

There wasn't much left after the fire so most of it was rebuilt as government offices, but the Royal Household Cavalry still mount guard at the Horse Guards building (above) in Whitehall.

ST JAMES'S PALACE This became the next official royal residence after Whitehall, and the Throne Room is still used for State occasions today.

The palace was built in 1531, also by Henry VIII. You can still see the carved initials of Henry and Anne Boleyn over the gatehouse doors facing into St James's Street. The last monarch to live at St James's was William IV, who died in 1837, but Prince Charles has offices there and stays there when he is in London.

1485–1509 HENRY VII IS THE FIRST TUDOR KING

1509–1547 HENRY VIII IS ON THE THRONE

1536 ACT OF UNION JOINS WALES WITH ENGLAND

KENSINGTON PALACE Sometimes the 'official residence' was used more for ceremonies than for living in. William III thought the air around Whitehall Palace was unhealthy so in 1689 he and his wife, Queen Mary, built a palace 'in the country' near the village of Kensington.

Kensington Palace remained a popular royal home until George III moved back to St James's Palace in 1760. Today, it is divided into apartments used by various members of the royal family.

Palace Parks

Many of London's largest parks were once palace gardens or hunting parks and are still owned and cared for by the Crown.

Hyde Park (one of Henry VIII's deer parks) and St James's Park were both opened to the public in the early 1600s.

Richmond Park was used for hunting by Charles I. The deer that live there today are descended from the original herds. The other royal parks are Greenwich Park, Green Park, Kensington Gardens, Regent's Park (including Primrose Hill) and Bushy Park.

WINDSOR CASTLE This is another favourite country retreat — and has been for hundreds of years. It was built by William the Conqueror, but a lot has been added to it since then. Windsor is the oldest royal home in Britain and, covering 13 acres, it's the largest castle in the world that is still lived in. It is used both as a royal home and sometimes for official State events.

HAMPTON COURT may be the most romantic royal house of all. Henry VIII had three of his six honeymoons there, and five of his wives lived their married lives there. In fact, one of them is still there! People say the screams of Catherine Howard as she was taken away to be executed are still sometimes heard in the Haunted Gallery.

1541
HENRY VIII
BECOMES KING
OF IRELAND

1547–1553
EDWARD VI
IS ON THE
THRONE

1553–1558
MARY I IS THE
FIRST WOMAN
TO RULE

Buckingham Palace

Today the main royal London home is **BUCKINGHAM PALACE**, although the Queen regularly spends time at Windsor Castle and at Balmoral Castle in Scotland.

The balcony above the main entrance to Buckingham Palace has become a favourite spot for the royal family to gather and be seen by the waiting crowds.

Another familiar sight at Buckingham Palace is the Changing of the Guard ceremony that takes place in the forecourt each morning. The monarch and the royal palaces have been guarded by the Household Troops since 1660.

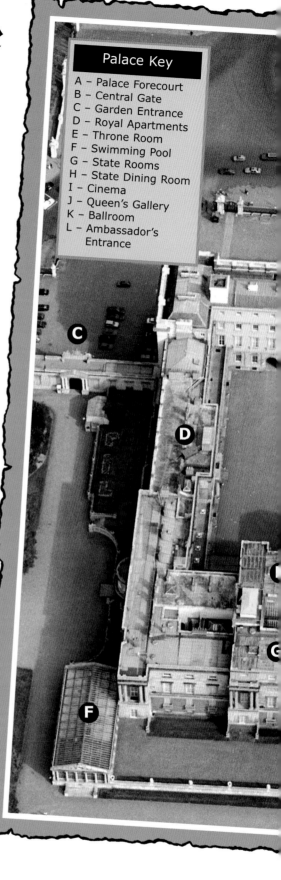

Palace Key

A – Palace Forecourt
B – Central Gate
C – Garden Entrance
D – Royal Apartments
E – Throne Room
F – Swimming Pool
G – State Rooms
H – State Dining Room
I – Cinema
J – Queen's Gallery
K – Ballroom
L – Ambassador's Entrance

1558–1603
ELIZABETH I
IS ON THE
THRONE

1603–1625
JAMES I
(JAMES VI OF
SCOTLAND)
IS KING

1603
JAMES I IS THE FIRST
KING OF ENGLAND,
SCOTLAND AND
WALES

Buckingham Palace

Buckingham Palace was originally a grand house. George III bought it in 1761 for £28,000. George IV began transforming it into a palace in 1826, and in 1837 Queen Victoria moved in.

The Palace has around 600 rooms, including 19 State rooms, 52 royal and guest bedrooms, 78 bathrooms, 92 offices, a cinema and a swimming pool. It also has its own post office and police station.

When Queen Elizabeth II is at home her flag, called the Royal Standard, flies from the flagpole above the main entrance.

MARBLE ARCH was originally built as a gateway to the central courtyard of Buckingham Palace. It was moved to Hyde Park in 1851 to make way for a fourth wing to be added to Buckingham Palace.

1625–1649
CHARLES I
IS ON THE
THRONE

1642–1649
ENGLISH CIVIL
WAR, ENDS WITH
EXECUTION OF
CHARLES I

The Royal Court

When Elizabeth I went travelling, she took a great many servants with her and more than 100 wagons full of household goods.

Throughout the Middle Ages, wherever the king or queen went, a vast army of guards, household servants, personal servants, companions, aides and officials went too. This was the royal court and everyone in it was fed and housed by the monarch, or sometimes by the unfortunate person the monarch chose to visit!

Leaders of fashion

The court was once the most powerful body in the land and even after Parliament took over the running of the country it still had enormous influence. Kings and queens and their courts set the fashion for everything from styles of clothing and furniture to music, dancing, art, or even manners!

Royal housework

Today, the members of the Queen's court are known as the Royal Household. There are about 650 people employed in the Household, ranging from the Queen's secretary to her footmen. Between them they handle all State and royal events, as well as taking care of the royal houses and estates.

Royal banquets are lavish affairs and take an enormous amount of organising by the Master of the Royal Household.

1649–1660
ENGLAND HAS NO KING OR QUEEN

1660–1685
CHARLES II IS ON THE THRONE

1665 AND 1666
THE GREAT PLAGUE IS FOLLOWED BY THE GREAT FIRE OF LONDON

A Knight's Tale

The first knights were mounted soldiers who came to England with William the Conqueror in 1066. Most knights fought for a richer, more powerful lord. In return, they were given land which provided them with a living and helped pay for their war horses and armour. In time, the term 'knight' came to mean a nobleman as well as a warrior.

None but the brave

Knighthoods were often given to young men on the battlefield when they had proved their bravery and ability to fight. By the 1200s, a knighthood was also a mark of honour. Knights were expected to be truthful, to defend the Church and to protect the weak.

Once, any knight could bestow a knighthood on another man simply by tapping him on the neck with a sword and saying "I dub you knight". Today, only the Queen can award a knighthood.

An Ancient Order

Nowadays, knighthoods are still seen as awards of honour and are given in recognition of service to the country. Most are given to people chosen by the Prime Minister, but there are some that only the Queen can decide to give. The highest of these (and the highest and most ancient of all the awards) is called the 'Order of the Garter'. It was founded by Edward III in 1348, and the King or Queen is always a Knight of the Garter. The patron saint of the Order is St George, and each knight's banner, helmet, sword and nameplate is hung in **St George's Chapel** at Windsor Castle.

685–1689
JAMES II
S ON THE
THRONE

1689
JAMES II DEPOSED.
THRONE GOES TO
HIS DAUGHTER
MARY

1689–1694
MARY II AND HER
HUSBAND
WILLIAM III RULE
TOGETHER

Royal Patrons

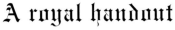

M any kings and queens liked to use their wealth and power to encourage clever or talented people (sometimes because it made them look clever too). They did this by becoming someone's patron and giving them work or gifts of money.

To show her support for innovations in electricity, Queen Victoria had electric lighting put in all her palaces.

The **ROYAL OBSERVATORY** was founded by Charles II at Greenwich in 1675 to discover a way for sailors to find their position accurately at sea (a puzzle that was not solved for another hundred years). The Observatory houses the country's largest refracting telescope and marks the famous line of 0° longitude from which the world's time zones are set.

A royal handout

E lizabeth I gave her favourite musicians positions at court and had her own group of actors, called 'Queen Elizabeth's Men'. (Unfortunately she also expected every member of her court to give her costly presents at least once a year!)

The merry monarch

C harles II loved dancing and theatre, but he also took a keen interest in the discovery of knowledge. He supported many writers, artists and inventors.

In 1660 he founded a club called the Royal Society which encouraged the growth and development of science. Its earliest members included some of the

The **ROYAL HOSPITAL CHELSEA** was also founded by Charles II. It was opened in 1692 as a retirement home for old soldiers who had been wounded in battle. Today about 360 Chelsea Pensioners live at the Hospital. In return, each one must attend the yearly Founder's Day celebration held in honour of Charles II. A member of the royal family always goes too.

1694–1702
WILLIAM III
RULES ALONE
AFTER MARY'S
DEATH

1702–1714
ANNE, MARY'S
SISTER, IS THE
LAST STUART
MONARCH

1707
ENGLAND, SCOTLAND
AND WALES BECOME
THE UNITED
KINGDOM

greatest thinkers of the time, such as the scientist Isaac Newton, and the astronomer Edmund Halley.

Builder George

George IV loved building things and gave his support to the planner John Nash, who designed a large part of London's West End, including Piccadilly Circus, Regent's Street and Oxford Circus.

In 1882, Edward VII (then the Prince of Wales) founded the **ROYAL COLLEGE OF MUSIC**, which is supported by the Queen and other members of the royal family today.

Between them the members of the royal family are patrons of a vast number of organisations and charities, supporting everything from the arts to youth training.

The Royal Collection

Over hundreds of years, kings and queens and other members of the royal family have gathered a priceless collection of art objects, including paintings, sculptures, furniture, silver, jewellery, books and armour. The suit of armour shown here, for example, belonged to Henry VIII.

The collection is not owned by the monarch but is held in trust by her on behalf of the nation. Most of the collection is on display in the public areas of the main royal palaces. There is a permanent exhibition of paintings and other objects in the **QUEEN'S GALLERY** at Buckingham Palace.

Queen Victoria's husband, Prince Albert, had a great enthusiasm for art and science, and for education. He helped buy the land on which some of London's finest museums were built, such as the **VICTORIA AND ALBERT MUSEUM**, the **SCIENCE MUSEUM** and the **NATURAL HISTORY MUSEUM** (left).

1714–1727
GEORGE I (OF HANOVER) IS ON THE THRONE

1727–1760
GEORGE II IS ON THE THRONE

1760–1820
GEORGE III IS ON THE THRONE

Royal Trades

In 1789, George III had a Pin Maker, a Mole Taker, a Card Maker and a Rat Catcher supplying services to his court.

The royal household has always needed a vast supply of everything from food to furniture polish to keep it going. All of these goods are bought from tradespeople, and to be chosen to supply something to the royal family is seen as an honour and a public 'stamp of approval'.

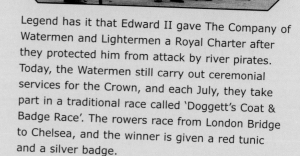

Legend has it that Edward II gave The Company of Watermen and Lightermen a Royal Charter after they protected him from attack by river pirates. Today, the Watermen still carry out ceremonial services for the Crown, and each July, they take part in a traditional race called 'Doggett's Coat & Badge Race'. The rowers race from London Bridge to Chelsea, and the winner is given a red tunic and a silver badge.

Licence to trade

In the Middle Ages, kings and queens gave (or sometimes sold) Royal Charters to groups of tradespeople or craftsmen called guilds. A Royal Charter gave a guild the right to control its particular trade and the prices of its goods or services. These guilds became very wealthy.

Up in Arms

Royal Warrants can be granted by four members of the royal family. Each has his or her own coat-of-arms:

HM Queen Elizabeth II

HRH Prince Philip
The Duke of Edinburgh

HRH Prince Charles
The Prince of Wales

HM Queen Elizabeth
the Queen Mother

Working warrants

Today, tradespeople may be given a Royal Warrant. These are granted to individual people or companies who have regularly supplied members of the royal family for at least five years.

Warrant holders can put a royal coat-of-arms on their products along with words "By Appointment". At present, there are about 800 Royal Warrant holders.

1800
ACT OF UNION
BRINGS IRELAND
INTO THE UNITED
KINGDOM

1820–1830
GEORGE IV
BECOMES KING
AT 54

1830–1837
WILLIAM IV
BECOMES KING
AT 64

The Inauguration, Plate 1 of 'The Great Industrial Exhibition of 1851', engraved by the artist, 1851 (colour litho) by Joseph Nash (1809-78)
Coram Foundation, Foundling Museum, London, UK/Bridgeman Art Library

The Great Exhibition

'The Great Exhibition of the Works of Industry of all Nations' of 1851 was the first international trade exhibition in the world and it was an enormous success. Prince Albert was so keen on the idea he raised the money to go ahead with it himself, from private supporters.

The Exhibition was held in Hyde Park, inside a gigantic hall made of glass and iron. Called the Crystal Palace, the hall was so big that living trees were enclosed inside it. The Exhibition opened on 1 May, and more than 6 million people visited it. Queen Victoria went 34 times in the first three months! People were amazed and fascinated by the thousands of exhibits from all over the world. There were all kinds of inventions, from steam engines to an early type of sewing machine, and objects made from every sort of material — including a fountain of glass and a garden bench carved from coal.

In 1852 the Crystal Palace was moved to Sydenham in south London. The area is still known as Crystal Palace, but the building itself burned down in 1936.

Prince Albert used the money raised by the Exhibition to buy the land in Kensington where many museums stand today. After his death, a grand statue called the **ALBERT MEMORIAL** was put up in his honour.

The statue of Prince Albert in the centre of the Albert Memorial holds a stone copy of the Exhibition's catalogue in its hands.

GUESS WHAT? Which king's wife pawned the Crown Jewels? a) Richard II's b) Henry VIII's c) Charles I's

1837–1901
VICTORIA, NIECE OF WILLIAM IV, BECOMES QUEEN AT 18

1840
WEDDING OF VICTORIA AND PRINCE ALBERT

Family of Nations

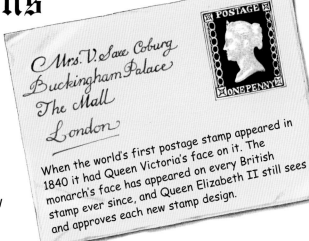

When the world's first postage stamp appeared in 1840 it had Queen Victoria's face on it. The monarch's face has appeared on every British stamp ever since, and Queen Elizabeth II still sees and approves each new stamp design.

When Queen Victoria came to the throne she was crowned Queen of Great Britain and Ireland. By the end of her reign she was queen of the largest empire the world had ever known.

The British Empire began as a few settlements in North America in the 1600s. But by 1900, it covered about one-fifth of all the world's lands and ruled over 370 million people. British people in their thousands went to live and work in these lands.

End of an empire

Victoria was very proud of the British Empire, but the two World Wars that followed her death saw the Empire crumble. By 1926, Australia, Canada, New Zealand, South Africa and most of Ireland had left the Empire and set up their own governments. At the same time, they became the first members of the 'Commonwealth of Nations' — a group of countries that share close trading and social links with Britain.

After 1945, India, Pakistan and many African and other countries also became independent. Some joined the Commonwealth but others left, such as the Republic of Ireland.

Being independent

Today, the Commonwealth is made up of 54 independent nations (including the United Kingdom) along with a number of territories and dependencies — parts of the world governed by one of the Commonwealth countries.

The growth of the British Empire was driven largely by the desire for new areas of trade. One of its richest sources of wealth was India. In 1877, Queen Victoria was thrilled to be made Empress of India.

1851
THE GREAT EXHIBITION IN HYDE PARK

1897
VICTORIA'S DIAMOND JUBILEE (60 YEARS ON THE THRONE)

1901-1910
EDWARD VII, VICTORIA'S SON, GAINS THRONE AT 59

Queen Elizabeth II is Head of the Commonwealth although she plays no part in the actual running of the Commonwealth countries. She often meets with the Heads of Government of Commonwealth countries and has visited every Commonwealth country at least once. Here, she is being welcomed by traditional dancers during her visit to Mozambique in 1999.

A Wealth of Knowledge

Together, the Commonwealth countries make up one quarter of the world's population. That's about 1.6 billion people, and over half of them are under the age of 25.

The COMMONWEALTH INSTITUTE in Kensington was set up to encourage awareness and understanding between the many different Commonwealth nations and their ways of life. The Institute runs education programmes in schools, holds public events and exhibitions, and houses a large resource centre.

A city of all sorts

Throughout its history London has been home to a lively and swirling mix of different nationalities. In ancient times, people came from every part of the Roman Empire to live and work in London.

In the 1200s, a monk wrote that London was 'overflowing' with Italians, Spanish and French, and in the 1500s many London trades depended on craftsmen and other workers from all over Europe.

In the 1900s, people from Asia and the Commonwealth countries came to live and work or study in London. Nowadays people come from all over the world, carrying on a tradition that has made London the bustling, vibrant city it is today.

1910-1936
GEORGE V
IS ON THE
THRONE

1914-1918
WORLD
WAR I

1921
MOST OF IRELAND
SEPARATES FROM
UNITED
KINGDOM

A Working Queen

Although the Queen is no longer responsible for governing the country, she carries out a great many important tasks on behalf of the nation.

Every day 'red boxes' are delivered to the Queen's desk full of documents and reports from government ministers and Commonwealth officials. They must all be read and, if necessary, signed by the Queen.

As Head of State, the Queen goes on official State Visits abroad. She also invites other world leaders to come to the United Kingdom. During their visit, Heads of State usually stay at Buckingham Palace, or sometimes at Windsor Castle or Holyroodhouse in Edinburgh. A State Banquet is given in their honour and they usually spend at least one day visiting different places around the country.

The Real Thing

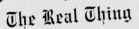

Portraits of kings and queens (like this one of King Alfred) have been engraved on coins for hundreds of years. But Queen Elizabeth II is the first monarch to have her portrait printed on a bank note. It was first done in 1960 as a way of helping to prevent forgeries.

I'm quite real you know!

The Queen is also Head of the Armed Forces. She is the only person who can declare when the country is at war and when a war is over, although she must take advice from her government about it first.

JAN–DEC 1936 EDWARD VIII, ELDEST SON OF GEORGE V, IS KING

DEC 1936 EDWARD VIII ABDICATES THE THRONE

1936–1952 GEORGE VI, SECOND SON OF GEORGE V, IS KING

A Fount of Justice

In ancient times, kings and queens were the final judges on matters of the law. They heard trials themselves and chose judges to act on their behalf. By the 1700s, monarchs no longer judged law cases, but when a new king or queen is crowned, he or she still swears to uphold the law and provide justice for all.

Because of this, the law courts still work 'in the Queen's name', and prisoners kept in Her Majesty's Prisons are held there 'during Her Majesty's pleasure', which is a traditional way of saying for as long as their sentence lasts.

The Queen cannot be taken to court herself, but 'the Crown' can. In this case, the Crown means the government or other official departments that act on behalf of the Queen.

At least three Royal Garden Parties are held at Buckingham Palace each year and about 8,000 guests attend each one.

The Queen also represents the nation at times of great celebration or sorrow. One example of this is the Remembrance Day ceremony at the Cenotaph monument in Whitehall. The Queen lays a wreath there each year to honour the members of the armed forces who have died fighting for their country.

Alongside her other duties, the Queen spends a huge amount of time travelling around the country visiting hospitals, schools, factories and other places and organisations.

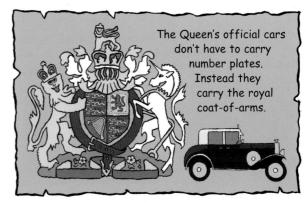

The Queen's official cars don't have to carry number plates. Instead they carry the royal coat-of-arms.

1939–1945 WORLD WAR II

1953 CORONATION OF QUEEN ELIZABETH II

2002 ELIZABETH II'S GOLDEN JUBILEE (50 YEARS ON THE THRONE)

Around Royal London

How much do you know about Royal London? Here's a list of the places you've read about in this book. Tick the box if you've been there; then see how many answers in our Royal London Quiz you can get right.

MARYLEBONE RD
EUSTON RD
EDGWARE RD
BAYSWATER RD
OXFORD ST
REGENT ST
PICCADILLY
CROMWELL RD
KINGS RD
BUCKINGHAM PALACE RD
CHELSEA EMBANKMENT

F

E D

B H

BATTERSEA PARK

ROYAL PARKS

A Bushy Park
B Green Park
C Greenwich Park
D Hyde Park
E Kensington Gardens
F Regent's Park
(including Primrose Hill)
G Richmond Park
H St James's Park

GREATER LONDON

A
G

1 Prince Albert's statue in the **Albert Memorial** is: a) 4 ft high b) 14 ft high c) 24 ft high

2 Charles I walked from **Banqueting House** to the scaffold through a: a) window b) door c) stairway

3 How many monarchs have lived at **Buckingham Palace**?: a) 2 b) 4 c) 6

4 The **Commonwealth Institute** is in: a) Fulham b) Kensington c) Mayfair

5 **Hampton Court** has a famous: a) maze b) tower c) bedroom

6 The entrance to **Horse Guards** forms the only official entrance to: a) Buckingham Palace b) St James's Palace c) Kensington Palace

7 The **Houses of Parliament** have more than:
a) 100 rooms b) 500 rooms c) 1,000 rooms

8 **Kensington Palace** was the birthplace of:
a) Queen Elizabeth I b) Queen Anne
c) Queen Victoria

9 **Marble Arch** was originally a gateway to:
a) Buckingham Palace b) St James's Palace
c) Whitehall Palace

10 The entrance to the Earth Galleries in the
Natural History Museum passes through a
model: a) mountain b) globe c) volcano

11 At the **Public Record Office** at Kew you can
see a copy of: a) the Domesday Book b) the *Magna
Carta* c) William Shakespeare's will

18

20

THE HIGHWAY

Some Royal Websites

The Queen and Buckingham Palace:
www.royal.gov.uk

Hampton Court and other palaces:
www.hrp.org.uk

St Paul's Cathedral:
www.stpauls.co.uk

Public Record Office:
www.pro.gov.uk

Westminster Abbey:
www.westminster-abbey.org

Queen Elizabeth II's Golden Jubilee
www.goldenjubilee.gov.uk

To find out all about London's history
check out the Museum of London at:
www.museum-london.org.uk

12 The **Queen's Gallery** used to be a:
a) kitchen b) stable c) chapel

13 The **Royal College of Music** has a museum
of: a) instruments b) sheet music c) costumes

14 The **Royal Hospital Chelsea** is a home for
retired: a) servants b) seamen c) soldiers

15 The **Royal Observatory, Greenwich,** was built
by: a) Charles I b) Charles II c) James I

16 **St George's Chapel** contains the tombs of:
a) 2 monarchs b) 5 monarchs c) 10 monarchs

17 Which queen was married at **St James's
Palace**?: a) Elizabeth I b) Victoria c) Elizabeth II

18 **St Paul's Cathedral** has been rebuilt at least:
a) five times b) three times c) once

19 In the **Science Museum** you can see: a) an
ant eater b) an Egyptian pyramid c) a meteorite

20 The **Tower of London** was built by:
a) William I b) Richard I c) Henry VIII

21 At the **Victoria and Albert Museum** you can
see: a) Prince Albert's slippers b) Queen Victoria's
hankie c) James II's wedding suit

22 The number of people buried in **Westminster
Abbey** is more than: a) 30 b) 300 c) 3000

23 Today, **Whitehall** is a: a) government building
b) road c) park

24 **Windsor Castle** was built by: a) William I
b) Henry VIII c) George IV

15

C

BLACKHEATH

31

Index

Albert Memorial 25, 30
Albert, Prince 15, 23, 25
Alfred the Great 4
Athelstan 4
Anne 5, 22

Banqueting House 11, 30
Buckingham Palace 18–19, 23,
    28, 29, 30, 31

Canute 4, 5
Changing of the Guard 18
Charles I 5, 11, 13, 17, 19
Charles II 5, 8, 11, 20, 22
Charles, Prince 15, 16
Church of England 10
Cromwell, Oliver 11
Commonwealth Institute 27, 30
Commonwealth of Nations 26, 27
Crown Jewels 9, 14

Edward I 5, 11
Edward II 5, 12, 24
Edward III 5, 9, 12, 21
Edward IV 5, 14
Edward V 5, 7, 8, 9, 15
Edward VI 5, 17
Edward VII 5, 23, 27
Edward VIII 5, 8, 28
Edward the Confessor 5, 6, 8, 9,
    16
Elizabeth I 5, 7, 18, 20, 22
Elizabeth II 5, 9, 10, 12, 13, 15,
    18, 19, 20, 23, 27, 28–29

George I & II 5, 23

George III 5, 17, 19, 23, 24
George IV 5, 19, 23, 24
George V 5, 27
George VI 5, 28
Great Exhibition, The 25

Hampton Court 16, 17, 30, 31
Harold I 5
Harold II 5, 6, 8
Henry I 5, 7, 8
Henry II 5, 8, 9
Henry III 5, 10
Henry IV & V 5, 13
Henry VI 5, 13, 14
Henry VII 5, 7, 16
Henry VIII 5, 7, 10, 12, 16, 17
Horse Guards 15, 16, 30
Houses of Parliament 12, 13, 31

James I 5, 18, 19
James II 5, 21
John 5, 9, 10, 11

Kensington Palace 17, 31

Magna Carta 10, 11
Marble Arch 19, 31
Mary I 5, 7, 17
Mary II 5, 17, 21

Natural History Museum 23, 31

Parliament 11, 12–13
Public Record Office 10, 31

Queen's Gallery 23, 31

Richard I 5, 9
Richard II 5, 12
Richard III 5, 7, 9, 15
Royal Charters and Warrants 24
Royal College of Music 23, 31
Royal Hospital Chelsea 22, 31
Royal Observatory 22, 31

St Edward's Crown 8, 9
St George's Chapel 21, 31
St James's Palace 16, 17, 31
St Paul's Cathedral 14, 15, 31
Science Museum 23, 31
Stephen 5, 7, 8

Tower of London 6, 9, 31
Trooping of the Colour 15

Victoria & Albert Museum 23, 31
Victoria, Queen 5, 14, 15, 19,
    22, 23, 25, 26

Westminster Abbey 8–9, 31
Westminster Palace 11, 12, 14, 16,
    see also Houses of Parliament
Whitehall 15, 16, 29, 31
Whitehall Palace 11, 16, 17
William I (the Conqueror) 5, 6,
    7, 8, 12, 17, 21
William II 5, 7
William III 5, 17, 21, 22
William IV 5, 16, 24
Windsor Castle 10, 17, 18, 21,
    28, 31

Quiz Answers

PAGE 5: c) A capital city is where a country is governed from. By the 1300s, the king's officials worked at Westminster and London had become the fixed seat of government.

PAGE 7: b) Prince Charles is the heir to the throne and Prince William comes next. Although Prince Philip is the Queen's husband he has no rights to the throne himself.

PAGE 9: b) 17 monarchs are buried in Westminster Abbey, including Mary I, Elizabeth I, and the bones found in the Tower that are believed to belong to Edward V.

PAGE 11: b) George II was the last king to lead troops into battle. He fought against the French in 1743.

PAGE 13: c) Henry VI was just 8 months old when he became king. Henry III was 9 years old and Richard II was 10 years old.

PAGE 15: a) 'God Save The King' was first performed in public at the Theatre Royal in London in 1745.

PAGE 17: b) None of the royal London palaces belong to the Queen although she uses them during her reign.

PAGE 19: b) George III had 15 legitimate children.

PAGE 21: a) Henry VI was 8 months old when he came to the throne in 1422. His coronation took place in 1429.

PAGE 23: b) Unlike most people of her time Elizabeth I had a bath four times a year 'whether she needed to or not'.

PAGE 25: c) Charles I's wife pawned the Crown Jewels for money to fight the Civil War. They were returned, but in 1649 Cromwell had them broken up and sold.

PAGE 27: c) George I was also the German King of Hanover. He spoke German but no English.

PAGE 29: a) 16 countries including the United Kingdom claim Elizabeth II as their queen, although all of them have their own separate governments. These countries range from Australia and Canada to the tiny group of Pacific islands called Tuvalu.

PAGES 30–31:
1b; 2a; 3c; 4b; 5a; 6b; 7c; 8c; 9a; 10b; 11a, b & c; 12c; 13a; 14c; 15b; 16c; 17b; 18a; 19c; 20a; 21c; 22c; 23b; 24a